W9-CBE-403

# Snow Day! Snow Play!

by Jenne Abramowitz
Illustrated by Jeff Ebbeler

SCHOLASTIC INC.

New York   Toronto   London   Auckland   Sydney
Mexico City   New Delhi   Hong Kong   Buenos Aires

Hear it! See it!
Falling from the sky.

Dancing snowflakes
float from way up high.

Twirling, swirling,
watch the white flakes fly!

# • RHYME • TIME • READERS •

## A Note to Parents

Rhyme, Repetition, and Reading are 3 R's that make learning fun for your child. **Rhyme Time Readers** will introduce your child to the sounds of language, providing the foundation for reading success.

### Rhyme

Children learn to listen and to speak before they learn to read. When you read this book, you are helping your child connect spoken language to written language. This increased awareness of sound helps your child with phonics and other important reading skills. While reading this book, encourage your child to identify the rhyming words on each page.

### Repetition

**Rhyme Time Readers** have stories that your child will ask you to read over and over again. The words will become memorable due to frequent readings. To keep it fresh, take turns reading and encourage your child to chime in on the rhyming words.

### Reading

Someday your child will be reading this book to you, as learning sounds leads to reading words and finally to reading stories like this one. I hope this book makes reading together a special experience.

*Have fun and take the time to let your child read and rhyme.*

*Francie Alexander*

—Chief Education Officer,
Scholastic's Learning Ventures

*For Lindsay and Haley—my inspiration*
*—J.A.*

*For James, Shannon, and Kiera*
*—J.E.*

ISBN-13: 978-0-545-01423-6
ISBN-10: 0-545-01423-9

Text copyright © 2008 by Jenne Abramowitz
Illustrations copyright © 2008 by Jeff Ebbeler

All rights reserved.   Published by Scholastic Inc.
SCHOLASTIC, RHYME TIME READERS,
and associated logos are trademarks
and/or registered trademarks of Scholastic Inc.

12  11  10  9  8  7  6  5  4  3  2  1               8  9  10  11 12  13/0

Printed in the U.S.A.
First printing, January 2008

Snow day? Let's play!
We race up the hill.

Slipping, sliding,
no way to stand still.

Sneaky, silent,
grab a bit of snow.

Cup it. Shape it.

Ready, steady, throw!

Head down, back turned,
then Mom catches sight.

Eyes wide. Can't hide...

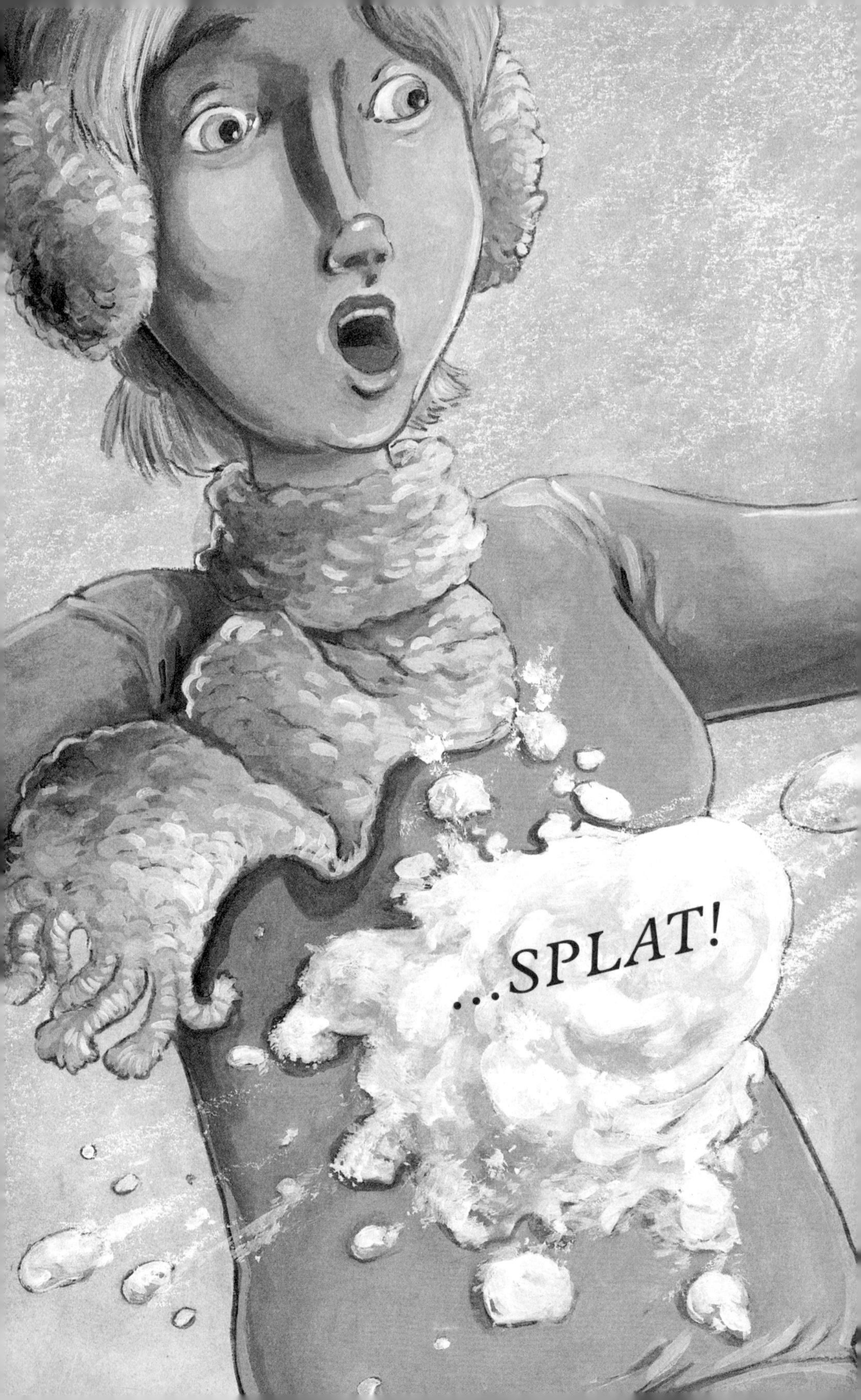
...SPLAT!

"Snowball fight!"

Arms high. Still dry.

Need more snowballs now.

Pack them. Stack them.

Doesn't matter how.

Mine hit. Dad's miss.
Haley has a plan.

Two balls in hand.
"Dodge them if you can!"

Dashing, ducking,
dive behind a tree.

Look left. Look right.
Can't let them get me!

One,

two,

three,

four

snowballs in the air.

Fall down laughing.
Snowflakes everywhere!

Arms out, legs wide,
angel in the snow.

Mom, Dad, Haley—
angels in a row.

Sun sets. Snow drips.
Winds begin to chill.

Time to head home,
down the icy hill.

Cuddle, huddle,
snuggle up with me.

Day's done.

Good fun

with my family.